ADVENTURES OF TOM SAWYER

Library of Congress Cataloging-in-Publication Data

Gise, Joanne.
   The adventures of Tom Sawyer.

   (Troll illustrated classics)
   Summary: The adventures and pranks of a mischievous
boy growing up in a Mississippi River town in the early
nineteenth century.
   [1. Mississippi River—Fiction. 2. Missouri—
Fiction] I. Twain, Mark, 1835-1910. Adventures of
Tom Sawyer. II. Burns, Raymond, 1924-   , ill.
III. Title.
PZ7.G446Af   1990   [Fic]   89-20559
ISBN 0-8167-1859-8 (lib. bdg.)
ISBN 0-8167-1860-1 (pbk.)

ADVENTURES OF TOM SAWYER

MARK TWAIN

Retold by
Joanne Gise

Illustrated by
Ray Burns

Troll Associates

"Tom!"

No answer.

"Tom! Where is that boy? TOM!"

The old lady pulled her glasses down and looked over them. Then she pushed them up and looked under them. She almost never looked *through* them. Loudly, she said, "If I get hold of you, I'll—"

She went to the open door and stood looking out into the garden. There was a slight noise behind her and she turned just in time to grab a boy by the back of his shirt and stop his flight.

"I might have known you were in that closet! What have you been doing in there?"

"Nothing, Aunt Polly."

"Nothing! Look at your hands. And look at your mouth. Forty times I've said if you didn't let that jam alone I'd skin you. Hand me that switch."

The switch hovered in the air. There was only one thing to do.

"Look behind you, Aunt!"

Aunt Polly whirled around. The boy fled, disappearing over the high board fence.

His aunt stood surprised a moment, then broke into laughter. "Can't I ever learn anything? He's played enough tricks like that. I know he'll play hooky today. I'll just have to make him work tomorrow, even if it is Saturday. He hates work more than anything, so that will punish him."

Tom did play hooky that day, and he had a very good time. But when Saturday morning came and all the world was bright and fresh and brimming with life, Tom was miserable. He appeared on the sidewalk with a bucket of whitewash and a long-handled brush. He looked at the fence, thirty yards long and nine feet high. Sighing, he dipped his brush and painted a few planks. He compared the whitewashed streak with the long stretch of unwhitewashed fence and sat down on a tree stump, discouraged.

Tom began to think of the fun he had planned for this day. Soon his friends would come along, and they would make fun of him for having to work. The very thought of it burned him. He searched through his pockets to see if he had enough treasures to trade for work. But the small assortment of marbles, toys, and bits of trash wasn't enough to buy him even half an hour of freedom.

Suddenly, a great inspiration struck him. Jumping to his feet, he went to work. Soon, Ben Rogers came along the road, munching happily on an apple. He stopped and stared at Tom, who kept on whitewashing as if he didn't know Ben was there.

"You're in a fix, aren't you?" Ben asked, grinning.

He got no answer. Tom looked at his work with the eye of an artist, then swept his brush gently along the fence. Ben drew closer.

"You've got to work, hey?" Ben asked.

Tom turned suddenly, as if surprised. "Why, hello, Ben! I didn't notice you at first."

"*I'm* going swimming," Ben informed him. "Don't you wish you could? But of course you'd rather *work,* wouldn't you?"

"What do you call work?" Tom asked him.

"Isn't *that* work?"

Tom resumed his whitewashing and answered carelessly, "Maybe it is and maybe it isn't. All I know is, it suits Tom Sawyer."

"Oh, come on. You don't mean to say that you *like* it?"

"Why shouldn't I like it? Does a boy get a chance to whitewash a fence every day?"

Ben had never thought of that. He stopped nibbling his apple. Tom swept his brush back and forth and stepped back to admire the effect. He added a touch here and there, then stepped back again.

Ben watched every move. Finally, he said, "Tom, let me whitewash a little."

"No, I'm afraid I can't, Ben. You see, Aunt Polly's very particular about this fence—it's right here on the street, you know. It's got to be done very carefully. I'll bet there isn't one boy in a thousand—maybe two thousand—who can do it the way it's got to be done."

"Really? Let me try. I'd let you, if it were me."

"Ben, I'd like to, honest, but Aunt Polly's awfully fussy."

"I'll be careful. Let me try. I'll give you the core of my apple."

"Well . . . no, I can't."

"I'll give you all of it."

Tom gave up the brush reluctantly, but his heart was glad. While Ben worked and sweated in the sun, Tom sat on a barrel in the shade close by, munching his apple and swinging his legs.

More boys came along. They jeered at first, but soon were lined up for a chance to whitewash. By the time Ben grew tired, Tom had traded his next chance to Billy Fisher for a kite. Then Johnny Miller wanted a turn and gave Tom a dead rat and a string to swing it on. And so it went, hour after hour. By the middle of the afternoon, Tom had twelve marbles, a piece of blue glass, a key that wouldn't unlock anything, a piece of chalk, a tin soldier, a couple of tadpoles, six firecrackers, a kitten with one eye, a brass doorknob, a dog collar, the handle of a knife, and four pieces of orange peel. And the fence had three coats of whitewash on it!

Tom said to himself that it was not such a bad world after all.

Aunt Polly was surprised when Tom presented himself to her that afternoon. She thought he had run off long ago.

"May I go and play now, Aunt?" Tom asked politely.

"Already? How much have you done?"

"It's all done."

"Tom, don't lie to me. You know it hurts me."

"I'm not lying. It *is* all done."

Aunt Polly went out to see for herself. She could hardly believe her eyes when she saw the entire fence beautifully whitewashed. "Well, Tom, I see you *can* work when you've a mind to," she said. "All right, go along and play. But try to get back sometime this week."

Tom ran off with a light heart and made his way through the village. As he passed by the house where Jeff Thatcher lived, he saw a new girl in the garden. She was lovely, with blue eyes and yellow hair braided into two long tails.

Tom began to show off for the girl without actually looking at her. He balanced on the fence, turned cartwheels, and did all sorts of dangerous stunts and tricks.

After a while, the girl walked up the path toward the house. Tom leaned against the fence, watching her. She started up the steps. Then she stopped and tossed a flower over the fence to him before she went inside.

Tom walked slowly toward the flower. He stopped to stare down the street as if something there interested him very much. Then he scooped up the flower and ran away.

All through supper that night, his spirits were so high that his aunt wondered what had gotten into him.

M onday morning found Tom miserable. Monday morning always found him this way, because it began another week's slow suffering in school.

As he made his way to school after breakfast, Tom met Huckleberry Finn. Huckleberry was the son of the town derelict. He was hated by all the mothers in town because all the children admired and envied Huckleberry's free and easy life. He came and went where and when he wanted, he did not have to go to school or church, he could stay up as late as he pleased, and he did not have to obey anybody.

Tom, like the other boys, was not allowed to play with Huckleberry. Of course, he played with him every chance he got. Now he called out, ''Hello, Huckleberry!''

''Hello, yourself, and see how you like it.''

''What's that you got?''

''Dead cat.''

''Let me see him. My, he's pretty stiff. What are dead cats good for, Huck?''

''Curing warts, of course.''

''Really? How do you do that?''

''You take your cat to the graveyard at night when somebody bad has been buried,'' Huck explained. ''When it's midnight, the devils come. You can't see them, but you can hear them. They sound like the wind blowing. When they're taking the dead fellow away, you throw your cat after them and say, 'Devil follow corpse, cat follow devil, warts follow cat, I'm done with you!' ''

"That sounds good. Did you ever try it?"

"No, but I'm going to tonight."

"Let me go with you."

"Sure—if you're not afraid."

"Afraid?" Tom laughed. "Meow at my window tonight, and I'll be ready."

Each boy went his separate way. When Tom reached the little schoolhouse, he walked in quickly, as if he had hurried all the way there. The schoolmaster's voice boomed out.

"Thomas Sawyer! Come up here. Why are you late again?"

Tom was about to lie when he saw the blonde braids of the new girl. At her side was the only empty seat on the girls' side of the schoolhouse. He instantly confessed, "I stopped to talk to Huckleberry Finn."

The master stared in disbelief. "Thomas Sawyer, that is the most astounding confession I have ever heard. For your punishment, you will go and sit with the girls."

The room rippled with laughter. Tom's cheeks flushed, not because of shame, but because he could not believe his good luck. He sat down at the edge of the bench. The new girl moved away with a toss of her head.

Tom sat still, intent on his book, until the attention of the other students had passed from him. Then he began to look at the girl. She looked away. When she looked back, a peach lay on the table in front of her. She pushed it away. Tom pushed it back. She thrust it away again, but not as hard as before. Tom returned it, and this time she let it stay.

Then Tom began to draw on his slate, hiding his work with his left hand. For a while, the girl refused to notice, but her curiosity got the better of her. ''Let me see it,'' she whispered.

Tom moved his hand to uncover a drawing of a house with a corkscrew of smoke trailing from the chimney. The girl forgot everything else. ''It's ever so nice,'' she whispered. ''I wish I could draw.''

''It's easy. I'll teach you,'' Tom whispered back.

''When?''

''At noon. What's your name?''

''Becky Thatcher.''

Now Tom began to scrawl something on the slate, hiding the words from the girl. But she begged to see it.

''It isn't anything,'' Tom said.

''Yes, it is. Please let me see it.''

''You won't tell anybody?''

''No, I won't ever tell. Now let me see.'' She put her hand on Tom's. Tom pretended to resist, but let his hand slip little by little until his words were revealed: ''I love you.''

''Oh, you bad thing!'' Becky blushed, but she looked pleased.

Just then, Tom felt a hard grip closing around his ear. The schoolmaster lifted Tom from his seat, carried him across the room, and deposited him none too gently in his seat. But although Tom's ear tingled, his heart was happy.

At half past nine that night, Tom was sent to bed. He lay awake and waited. When it seemed to him that hours had gone by, he heard the hall clock strike ten! Tom groaned. He lay staring into the dark. Slowly, he began to hear all the little noises of the night. Old beams cracked mysteriously. The stairs creaked. A cricket chirped. The howl of a far-off dog rose on the night air.

Tom began to doze. The clock struck eleven, but he didn't hear it. Then, a terrible wailing disturbed his dreams. "Meow-w-w!"

In a minute, Tom was dressed and out the window. He crept along the roof on all fours, meowing as he went. Finally, he jumped to the ground. Huckleberry Finn was there with his dead cat. The boys moved off into the gloom. A half hour later, they were at the graveyard.

The graveyard was on a hill, about a mile and a half from the village. It had a crazy board fence around it, which leaned inward in places and outward in others. Grass and weeds grew over the whole cemetery.

A faint wind moaned through the trees. Tom feared it was the spirits of the dead, complaining of being disturbed. The boys talked little, and only in whispers. Soon they found the newly dug grave they were seeking and settled down to wait behind the protection of three great elms that grew a few feet away from the grave. The hooting of a distant owl was the only sound. Then—

"Listen!"

A muffled sound of voices floated up from the end of the graveyard.

"Look!" Tom whispered. "What is it?"

"It's devil-fire. Oh, this is awful!"

Vague figures appeared through the gloom, swinging lanterns that freckled the ground with bits of light. "It's the devils, sure enough," Huckleberry whispered with a shudder. "Tom, we're goners!"

"Don't worry. They won't hurt us. I—"

"Shh! Tom, they're not devils. They're humans! I hear Muff Potter's voice! Don't move. He's probably drunk, and he'll never notice us."

"All right. Say, Huck, I know another one of those voices. It's Injun Joe!"

"You're right. I'd rather meet a devil than him. What can they be up to?"

Tom didn't answer, for the men—there were three of them—had reached the grave and stood only a few feet from the boys' hiding place.

"Here it is," said the third man. He held up the lantern to reveal the face of young Doctor Robinson.

Potter and Injun Joe were carrying a wheelbarrow with a rope and a couple of shovels. They put their load down and began to open the grave. Tom realized they were going to rob it.

The doctor put his lantern at the head of the grave and sat down with his back against one of the elm trees. "Hurry!" he said in a low voice.

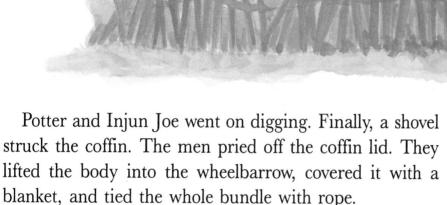

Potter and Injun Joe went on digging. Finally, a shovel struck the coffin. The men pried off the coffin lid. They lifted the body into the wheelbarrow, covered it with a blanket, and tied the whole bundle with rope.

Muff Potter took out a large knife and cut off the dangling end of the rope. "Give us more money," he demanded of the doctor, "or we don't go any further."

"That's right," Injun Joe growled.

The doctor stood up. "I paid you already," he said.

"You've done more than that!" shouted Injun Joe. "Five years ago, you drove me away from your father's kitchen when I came begging for food, and your father had me arrested for being a vagrant. Now you'll pay for that!" He waved his fist in the doctor's face.

The doctor struck out suddenly and knocked Injun Joe to the ground. Muff Potter dropped his knife. "Don't you hit my partner!" he shouted. The next moment, he and the doctor were rolling around on the ground.

Injun Joe jumped to his feet, his eyes flaming. He snatched up the knife and crept around the fighters, waiting.

All at once, the doctor flung himself free, seized the heavy wooden grave marker, and hit Potter over the head with it. As Potter fell, Injun Joe saw his chance and drove the knife into the young doctor's chest. The doctor fell on top of Potter. Then the clouds blotted out the moon that lit the dreadful sight, and the two frightened boys raced away in the dark.

om and Huckleberry were so afraid of Injun Joe that they swore never to tell anyone what they had seen. So it wasn't until noon of the next day that word of the murder reached the village. School was dismissed early, and the children, along with just about everyone else in town, headed for the graveyard.

Word was that a bloody knife found near the body had been recognized as Muff Potter's. Even now, the sheriff had men looking for him.

Tom met Huckleberry at the graveside. Injun Joe, to their horror, was also there. Then voices on the edge of the crowd began to shout, ''It's him! Muff Potter!'' The sheriff came through, leading Muff Potter by the arm. The poor man's eyes were wide with fear. When he stood before the body, he burst into tears.

''I didn't do it!'' he cried. ''On my word, I didn't do it!''

''Is this your knife?'' demanded the sheriff. Potter couldn't deny that it was.

Then Huckleberry and Tom stood in stunned silence while Injun Joe told a long and detailed story of how Muff Potter had killed the doctor in the fight last night. The boys fully expected lightning to strike the black-hearted liar. But nothing happened. And when Injun Joe had finished and stood still alive and whole, their impulse to break their oath and save poor, betrayed Muff Potter vanished. Obviously, Injun Joe was an even mightier foe than they'd thought. And so Muff Potter was led away to jail for a crime he hadn't committed.

Tom was miserable. Not only was he filled with guilt over the events at the graveyard, but Becky Thatcher and he had quarrelled, and she refused to speak to him. He felt he was a friendless boy; clearly no one loved him. There was only one thing to do. He would become a pirate.

And so, instead of heading for school one morning, Tom went in the opposite direction. He soon met Joe Harper, his best friend. Joe had a terrible look on his face. His mother had punished him for drinking some cream he had never tasted. Obviously, she was tired of him and wouldn't miss him if he ran away.

Tom told Joe of his idea. The two made a pact to stand by each other and become pirates. Then they found Huckleberry Finn. He was eager to join them in their adventure.

Three miles from their village, at a point where the Mississippi River was just over a mile wide, there was a long, narrow, wooded island called Jackson's Island. No one lived there, so it seemed the perfect place for the pirates to set up their camp. There was a small raft tied along the riverbank they could use to sail to their pirate's cove. The boys agreed to meet at midnight, bringing any food they could steal from home.

That night, the Black Avenger of the Spanish Main, Finn the Red-Handed, and the Terror of the Seas—also known as Tom, Huck, and Joe—met to begin their adventure. Taking the raft, they set out into the river. Some two hours later, they grounded the raft on the sandbar above the head of the island and carried their freight ashore. Part of the little raft's belongings was an old sail. They spread it over a nook in the bushes for a tent to shelter their provisions. They themselves would sleep in the open in good weather, as outlaws should.

They built a fire against the side of a great log twenty or thirty steps within the somber depths of the forest, and cooked some of the bacon they'd brought. It seemed quite a sport to be feasting in this wild, free way, and they said they would never return to civilization.

When the last crisp slice of bacon was gone, the boys stretched themselves out on the grass. "Isn't this great?" said Joe.

"It is," said Tom. "What would the boys say if they could see us?"

"Why, they'd just die to be here!"

"I'm happy," said Huckleberry. "I don't want anything better than this. I don't usually get enough to eat, and here no one can bully me."

"It's just the life for me," said Tom. "You don't have to get up, and you don't have to go to school, and wash, and all that other nonsense. A pirate doesn't have to do *anything* he doesn't want to."

Gradually, their talk died out and they grew sleepy. Finn the Red-Handed slept soundly. But the Terror of the Seas and the Black Avenger could not fall asleep, for their consciences were wide awake. They began to feel a vague fear that they had done wrong to run away. Then they thought of the meat they had stolen, and things grew worse. They tried to tell themselves that they had taken sweets and apples scores of times. But taking sweets was one thing. Taking bacon and ham was plain and simple stealing. So they promised themselves that they would never steal again, as long as they were pirates. Then, their consciences at peace for now, they fell asleep.

The pirates had marvelous fun on the island the next day. They swam and fished and explored to their hearts' content. They felt no longing for the village. During the night, the current had carried off their raft, but this only pleased them. It seemed as if they had burned their last bridge to civilization.

That afternoon, they became aware of a deep booming noise in the distance.

"What is it?" asked Joe.

"It isn't thunder," Huck said.

Again, the muffled boom broke the solemn hush.

"Let's go and see!" Tom cried.

They sprang to their feet and hurried to the shore toward town. Peering through the bushes, they could see the ferryboat on the river, about a mile below the village. There were many small boats floating around the ferryboat, but the boys could not see what the men in them were doing. A huge puff of white smoke burst from the ferryboat's side and that dull explosion came across the water again.

"I know now!" exclaimed Tom. "Someone's drowned!"

"That's it!" said Huck. "They did that last summer when Bill Turner drowned. They shoot a cannon over the water and that makes the body come to the top."

"I wish I was over there now," Joe said.

"I do, too," said Huck. "I'd give anything to know who it is."

The boys listened and watched for a while longer. Then Tom exclaimed, "I know who's drowned—it's us!"

They felt like heroes in an instant. What a triumph! They were missed, hearts were broken because of them, tears were being shed, and best of all, they were the talk of the whole town.

As twilight drew on, the ferryboat went back to its usual business and the pirates returned to camp. They were excited beyond measure over their new importance and the trouble they were making in town.

But when the shadows of night closed around them, their conversation ended. The boys sat staring into the fire, their minds wandering. The excitement was gone. Tom and Joe could not stop thinking of the people at home who were not enjoying the fun.

After a while, Joe and Huck fell asleep. Tom lay watching them for some time. At last, he got up and found a piece of bark. On it he scrawled, "We are only off being pirates." Slipping it into his pocket, he tiptoed into the trees until he was out of hearing. Then he broke into a run toward the sandbar.

It was very late when Tom came to his aunt's house. He had reached the village by swimming to the ferryboat and then stowing away for the short trip up the river. Now he looked in the sitting room window and saw Aunt Polly, his cousin Mary, and Joe Harper's mother grouped together, talking.

Tom crept quietly through the door and into the house. The bed was between the door and the group, and Tom ducked under it before anyone could see him. There he lay and listened to his aunt talk about him. Oh, the kind and wonderful things she said about him! How she loved him and missed him, now that she would never see him again! Tom was so touched by his aunt's grief that he longed to burst from his hiding place and overwhelm her with joy. But he forced himself to lay still.

He went on listening, and heard that the boys were thought to have drowned when the raft was found empty about five miles from the village. It was thought their bodies must have drifted away in the strong current. If they were not found by Sunday, all hope would be given up and their funerals would be held that morning.

After everyone had left, Aunt Polly went to bed and fell into a restless sleep. Tom got out from under the bed and looked at her. His heart was full of pity. As he stood there, a marvelous idea occurred to him. Instead of leaving his piece of bark, he bent over and kissed his aunt's lips. Then he slipped out of the house and back to the island.

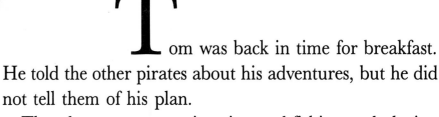

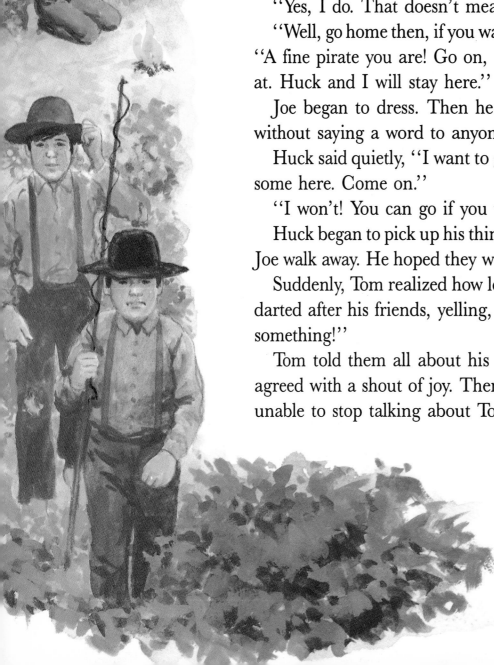

Tom was back in time for breakfast. He told the other pirates about his adventures, but he did not tell them of his plan.

That day was spent swimming and fishing and playing marbles. But when night came, loneliness and homesickness again settled over the pirates. Suddenly, Joe announced that he wanted to go home.

"Baby!" Tom teased him. "You want to see your mother!"

"Yes, I do. That doesn't mean I'm a baby."

"Well, go home then, if you want!" Tom said with scorn. "A fine pirate you are! Go on, go home and get laughed at. Huck and I will stay here."

Joe began to dress. Then he walked toward the shore without saying a word to anyone.

Huck said quietly, "I want to go, too, Tom. It's too lonesome here. Come on."

"I won't! You can go if you want to. I mean to stay."

Huck began to pick up his things. Tom watched him and Joe walk away. He hoped they would stop, but they didn't.

Suddenly, Tom realized how lonely and quiet it was. He darted after his friends, yelling, "Wait! I want to tell you something!"

Tom told them all about his secret plan, and the boys agreed with a shout of joy. Then they came back happily, unable to stop talking about Tom's wonderful idea.

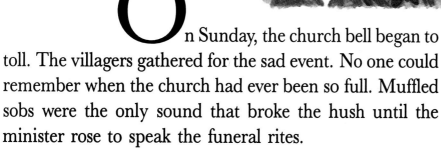

On Sunday, the church bell began to toll. The villagers gathered for the sad event. No one could remember when the church had ever been so full. Muffled sobs were the only sound that broke the hush until the minister rose to speak the funeral rites.

As the minister spoke of all the virtues and wonderful deeds of the dead boys, more and more people began to cry. At last, everyone present was sobbing. Even the minister cried in the pulpit.

There was a rustle in the gallery and the creaking of a door. The minister looked up and stood staring in disbelief. First one, then another pair of eyes followed his gaze. Then everyone rose and stared while the three dead boys marched down the aisle. They had hidden in the unused gallery and listened to their own funeral!

Aunt Polly, Mary, and the Harpers threw themselves upon Tom and Joe, smothering them with kisses. Poor Huck stood alone and uncomfortable, for no one seemed to care that he was back. Finally, Tom said, "Aunt Polly, it isn't fair. Somebody's got to be glad to see Huck."

"I'm glad to see him, poor motherless thing," said Aunt Polly.

Tom Sawyer looked around at everyone and confessed to himself that this was the proudest moment of his life.

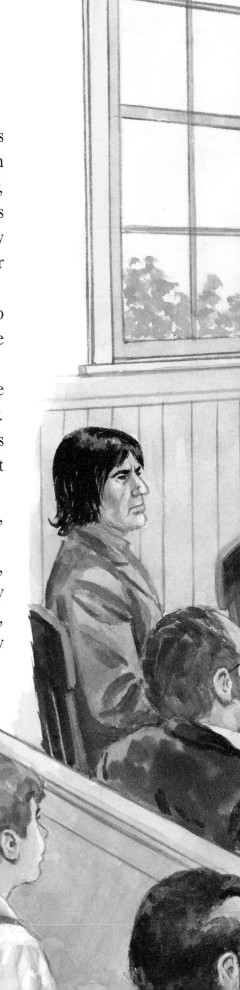

At last it was time for Muff Potter's murder trial. This was now the main topic of conversation in the village. Any time anyone mentioned the murder, Tom would shudder. His troubled conscience and fears almost convinced him that everyone was aware he knew something about the murder. It kept him in a cold shiver all of the time.

Tom hung around the courtroom. He half-wanted to go inside, but forced himself not to. Huck was having the same experience. They avoided one another.

Tom kept his ears open when spectators came out. He learned that things did not look good for poor Muff Potter. At the end of the second day, talk was that Injun Joe's evidence was unshaken and there was not the slightest question that the jury would return a guilty verdict.

Tom stayed out very late that night. When he came home, he was so excited he could not get to sleep for hours.

All the village was at the courthouse the next morning, for this was to be a great day. After a long wait, the jury filed in and took their places. Muff Potter was brought in, pale, thin, and in chains. Injun Joe was there, too. Finally the judge entered and the court was called to order.

Witness after witness testified that Potter had been seen acting strangely the morning of the murder and that his knife had been found near the body. Potter's lawyer did not question any of these witnesses.

Finally, it was Potter's lawyer's turn to call witnesses. He said, "Call Thomas Sawyer!"

Amazement was clear on every face, including Potter's, as Tom took the stand. He looked badly scared, but his conscience was clear. The night before, he had gone to Potter's lawyer and told what he knew.

Now Tom told his story of how he was in the graveyard the night of the murder, hiding behind the elms near the robbed grave. The tale spilled out of him, and everyone in the audience hung upon his words. Then, just as Tom was saying, " —and as the doctor brought the board around and Muff Potter fell, Injun Joe jumped with the knife and—" there was a tremendous crash! Quick as lightning, Injun Joe jumped for the window, pushed his way through those who tried to stop him, and was gone!

Injun Joe could not be found, but Tom was the hero of the village once more. He drank in all the attention, strutting and posing. But soon he was ready for another adventure. He found Huck Finn, and the two boys decided to go digging for buried treasure.

"Where should we dig?" Huck asked.

Tom thought for a few minutes. Then he said, "I know! The haunted house!"

And so, the boys set off for the haunted house. The house was so gloomy and silent, so lonely and depressing, that for a moment they were afraid to go inside. Then they crept to the door and peered in. They saw a weed-grown, floorless room, an ancient fireplace, empty windows, a ruined staircase, and, everywhere, ragged cobwebs. Finally, they entered, listening carefully for any strange sound.

But after a while they grew bolder and began to explore the house. They even ventured upstairs, leaving their pick and shovel in a corner downstairs. Then, just as they were about to go down and start digging, they heard voices coming up the path into the house!

The boys stretched out on the floor with their eyes to knotholes in the planking. They lay very still, frozen with fear.

Two men entered the house. One was an old deaf and dumb Spaniard who had lately been hanging around town. The other was a ragged, unpleasant-looking man neither boy recognized. The men sat down facing the door and the ragged one began to speak.

"I don't want to do it," he said. "I've thought it over and it's too dangerous."

"Dangerous!" said the deaf and dumb Spaniard, to the boys' great surprise. Their surprise turned instantly to fear when they recognized the voice. The "deaf and dumb Spaniard" was really Injun Joe!

"It's no more dangerous than that last job," Injun Joe continued. "I'll tell you what. You go back up the river and wait there until you hear from me. I'll take a chance and drop into town for one last look. We'll do that 'dangerous' job when things look right for it. Then we'll head for Texas!"

The other man agreed.

"Let's move on," Injun Joe said. "What do you want to do with the money we have left?"

"Let's leave it here. We won't need it until we start for Texas, and six hundred in silver is heavy to carry."

"All right. We'll bury it deep."

"Good idea," said his partner. Injun Joe began to dig in the corner with his knife.

The boys forgot all their fears. They watched every movement below with eager eyes. What luck! Six hundred dollars was enough to make half a dozen boys rich! Here was the best kind of treasure hunting—they would know exactly where to dig!

Injun Joe's knife struck something. "What's this?" he said. "A box." He pulled the object out. "It's full of money!" he exclaimed.

The two men examined the coins they'd found. They were gold! Up above, the boys were just as excited and delighted.

"There's thousands of dollars here," said Injun Joe.

"It was always said that Murrel's gang was here one summer. This must be their loot. Now we don't have to do that other job."

Injun Joe frowned. "You don't know me. That other job isn't just robbery. It's *revenge*. I'll need your help to do it. Go home for now, and wait until you hear from me."

"If you say so. What'll we do with this? Bury it again?"

"Yes," Injun Joe said. The boys were delighted. But their hearts fell as he said, "No! Look at that pick and shovel over there. They weren't here before. Who could have brought them here, and where are they now? Why should we bury the money again for them to take? No, we'll take it to our other place, under the cross."

"All right. Let's go. It's getting dark."

Injun Joe got up and walked from window to window, peering outside. "Who could have brought those tools here?" he said. "Do you think whoever it is could be upstairs?"

The boys' breath left them. Injun Joe put his hand on his knife, halted a moment, then turned toward the stairway. Tom and Huck were in an agony of terror as steps came creaking up the stairs. There was nowhere to hide!

CRASH! The rotten timbers of the stairs gave out and Injun Joe landed on the ground amid the debris of the ruined staircase.

"Let's go," his partner said. "There's no one up there. And there's only fifteen minutes left before dark."

Injun Joe agreed, grumbling, and the two men left, taking their precious box with them.

It was a relieved and angry Tom and Huck who made their way down the remains of the staircase. If only they hadn't left their tools downstairs, Injun Joe would have left the treasure there and they could have claimed it for themselves! They resolved to look for "the Spaniard" in town and follow him, in hopes of claiming the treasure once again.

Becky Thatcher's mother said she could have a picnic, and all her schoolfriends were invited. The old steam ferryboat was chartered for the occasion. Three miles below town, the boat stopped at the mouth of a woody hollow. The crowd of children swarmed ashore, and soon the woods and hills echoed far and near with shouts and laughter.

Finally, the hot and tired group stumbled back to camp and ate their fill of the good food awaiting them. Then, after resting a bit, somebody shouted, "Who's ready for the cave?"

Everybody was ready to explore McDougal's Cave. It was a popular place. Candles were gathered, and the group raced up the hill. The massive oaken door at the mouth of the cave was open. Inside was a small chamber, walled by nature with solid limestone. The walls were dewy with moisture.

It was romantic and mysterious to sit here in the gloom and look out on the green valley shining in the sun. But it was not long before the real exploring began. Eventually, the procession was filing down the steep descent of the main avenue. Lofty walls of rock towered sixty feet overhead.

Every few steps along the main path there were other, narrower pathways that branched off. McDougal's Cave was really a vast labyrinth of crooked paths that led nowhere. It was said that one might wander this tangle of pathways and never find the end of the cave. No one knew all of the cave, but parts of it were familiar enough. The group stayed on these well-known paths.

The children split into smaller groups to explore. By and by, one group after another straggled to the mouth of the cave. They were laughing, tired, and filthy from the candle drippings and the wet walls. The children were astonished to find that they had been underground for a long time and that night was nearly upon them. Everyone made their way to the boat. The ferry headed home with her tired crew.

It wasn't until the next morning that everyone realized Tom and Becky had not returned.

While the children were having a fine time at the picnic, Huckleberry Finn was having an adventure of his own. He had been watching around town for the past few nights, and this night he was rewarded with the sight of Injun Joe and his partner making their stealthy way down the street. Injun Joe had a box under his arm. Huck thought it was the box of gold. He decided to follow them, trusting the darkness to hide him.

They moved up the street, then made their way up the path on Cardiff Hill. Past Mr. Jones' house they walked. Huck thought they were going to bury the treasure in the old quarry on the hill. But they passed that, too.

Suddenly, the men plunged into a narrow path between the bushes. Huck followed. When the men stopped, they were at the entrance to the Widow Douglas' property. Were they going to bury the treasure here?

Injun Joe spoke. ''There are lights on in the house. She must have company.''

A chill went through Huck. This must be the ''revenge'' job the men had spoken of that day in the haunted house. And the box Injun Joe was carrying must contain, not the treasure, but tools to break into the widow's house! Huck was about to run away, then remembered that the Widow Douglas had been kind to him several times. He wanted to run and warn her, but he knew the men would see him. So he stayed where he was.

"Give it up," the other man said.

"Give it up!" Injun Joe replied. "Give it up and maybe never have another chance! No. Her husband was rough on me. He was the justice of the peace that had me jailed for being a vagrant. He's dead now, but I'll take it out on *her*. And if you don't help me, I'll kill you. Do you understand?"

"Well, if it's got to be done, let's do it."

"Not now, while company's there. No, we'll wait until the lights go out. There's no hurry."

A deep silence fell. Huck dared to move. He backed away carefully, quietly, then turned and walked quickly down the path. When he came to the quarry, he broke into a run and did not stop until he reached Mr. Jones' house. He pounded on the door until the man and his sons let him in.

When the men heard Huck's story, they gathered up their guns and headed up the path. Huck followed far enough to hear the explosion of pistol shots that followed.

But the villains had not been caught. The men chased them into the woods, firing, but none of their shots found its mark. Finally, the sheriff was alerted. A search would be started at daylight. An exhausted Huck was sent off to sleep in Mr. Jones' spare bed.

Tom and Becky had walked the familiar aisles of the cave with everyone else, but had somehow wandered away from the others. By the time they realized their mistake, they were hopelessly lost.

The cave was so silent around them that even their breathing sounded loud. Tom shouted, but his call only echoed down the empty aisles like a ripple of mocking laughter. There was no answer.

The children walked on and on. At last, they could go no further. Becky cried for a while. Then she slept. When she woke, the two traveled on again. They hoped to stumble on a familiar path, but they did not.

Finally, the sound of dripping water brought them to a spring. "This is our last piece of candle," Tom told Becky gently. "We must stay where there is water to drink."

After a while, Becky said, "They'll miss us, and hunt for us, won't they, Tom?"

"Of course they will!" The thought fired him with new hope.

"Maybe they're hunting for us now!"

"I'm sure they are." But the air around them was still. There were no sounds of feet in the distance, no voices calling their names.

Their candle melted slowly away. Finally, the feeble flame flickered and then went out! Complete darkness settled around them.

Tom decided to explore the side passages near the spring. It would be better than sitting and doing nothing. And so, tying a bit of kite line he found in his pocket to a rock, Tom and Becky walked along, unwinding the line as they went.

They had only gone twenty steps when the passage ended in a "jumping-off place," as Tom called it. He knelt down and reached his arm down to feel around. He stretched as far as he could to the right. At that moment, a human hand, holding a candle, appeared from behind a rock not twenty yards away!

Tom let out a joyful shout. They were saved!

Then the hand was followed by the body it belonged to. It was Injun Joe!

Tom was so frozen with fear, he could not move. If Injun Joe recognized his voice, he would kill Tom for testifying against him at the trial.

But Injun Joe turned and ran off. Tom realized that the echoes must have disguised his voice. Shaking with relief, Tom told Becky he had only shouted for luck. The two went back to the spring and waited in the darkness for help that might never come.

A long time passed. Tom grew restless and wanted to explore some more, but Becky was too weak to go with him. So he left her sleeping and went off on his own.

He went down two paths as far as his kite line would reach. But they led nowhere, and he was forced to turn back. A third path seemed just as hopeless. Then, just as he was about to turn around, Tom saw a faint glimmer of light!

Tom dropped the string and ran toward the light. He pushed his head and shoulders through a small hole and saw the Mississippi River flowing by.

Tom ran back and woke Becky, and together they made their way outside. Two men sailing by in a rowboat found them and brought them back to town. They had been missing for three days and were five miles below the cave entrance, but they were free!

In the middle of the night, the village bell began to ring. In a moment, the streets were filled with people shouting, ''They're found! They're found!'' The crowd swarmed down to the river to meet the children.

Tom and Becky were carried to Judge Thatcher's house. No one slept that night, for they all wanted to see the children and welcome them home.

Tom heard all about the adventure at the Widow Douglas' house, as well as the escape of the robbers. There was no sign of Injun Joe, but his partner's body had been found in the river. He had apparently drowned while trying to escape.

About two weeks after Tom's rescue, he went to see Becky. He chatted a while with the judge, who happened to mention that no one would ever be able to get into the cave again.

"Why not?" Tom asked.

"Because I had the door at the entrance triple locked with the strongest iron—and I've got the only keys."

Tom turned as white as a sheet. "Judge," he gasped, "Injun Joe's in the cave!"

This news spread through the town like lightning. Soon, boats full of the curious were on their way to McDougal's Cave.

When the cave door was unlocked, a terrible sight presented itself. Injun Joe lay stretched out on the ground, dead, his face pressed to the crack of the door.

The morning after Injun Joe's funeral, Tom took Huckleberry aside for an important talk. "Huck," he said, "I know where the money is! It's in the cave!"

And so the boys set off. They borrowed a boat and sailed down the Mississippi to the spot where Tom and Becky had escaped from the cave. They had with them some food, kite strings, candles, matches, and several bags.

The boys made their way into the cave, Tom in the lead. A few steps brought them to the spring, then down the hallway to the "jumping-off place." The candles revealed that this was not a cliff, as Tom had thought in the dark. It was really a steep hill about twenty feet high.

Tom lifted his candle. "Look at that big rock, Huck. What do you see marked there with candle smoke?"

"Tom, it's a *cross*! Injun Joe said he was going to hide the money under a cross!"

"That's right. And that's the spot where I saw Injun Joe poke up his candle. The money must be buried in the clay under that rock."

Tom took out his knife and began to dig. He hadn't gone more than four inches when he struck wood.

The treasure was there, all right. Tom could lift the box out, but it weighed about fifty pounds, so he could not carry it. He was glad they'd brought the bags along. The money was soon packed in the bags and carried out of the cave.

It was after dark by the time they returned to the village. They decided to hide the money in the loft of the Widow Douglas' woodshed until later, when they would find a better hiding place in the woods. Tom borrowed a wagon to carry it.

But as they were on their way up the hill, Mr. Jones came out of his house and saw them.

"Come along with me," he said. "Everyone is waiting for you."

"What do you mean?" Tom asked.

"The widow is having a big party. And she has an announcement to make."

Indeed, everyone in the village was there. The widow had even laid out new suits of clothes for the boys to wear, much to their great discomfort.

At the party, the widow announced that she wanted to reward Huck for his part in saving her from the robbers. From now on, Huck would have a home under her roof and would go to school. She said that she hoped to one day have enough money to set him up in business.

At that, Tom spoke up. "Huck doesn't need it," he said. "Huck's rich."

Everyone smiled. Tom went on. "Maybe you don't believe it, but I can show you. Just wait a minute."

He ran outside. Huck sat tongue-tied until Tom returned, struggling under the weight of the sacks. He poured the mass of yellow coins upon the table and said, "There. What did I tell you? Half of it's Huck's and half of it's mine."

The sight of all that gold took everyone's breath away. Then everyone called for an explanation, which Tom cheerfully gave. When the gold was finally counted, it added up to over twelve thousand dollars!

Tom and Huck's discovery made quite a stir in the sleepy little town. So vast a sum, all in cash, seemed incredible. Wherever Tom and Huck appeared, they were admired and stared at.

The Widow Douglas invested Huck's money, and Judge Thatcher did the same for Tom. The judge had a high opinion of Tom and thought him a fine companion for his daughter.

Huck Finn was now under the Widow Douglas' care, and he hated it. He had to be clean and neat all the time, eat with a knife and fork, use a napkin, go to church, and talk like a gentleman. It seemed that everywhere he turned, the chains of civilization bound him hand and foot.

Huck bravely bore his miseries for three weeks. Then he ran away. For two days, everyone in town searched for him, but he could not be found. It was Tom who went down to an abandoned building and found Huck eating some food he had stolen. He was dirty and ragged and very happy.

Tom told Huck of the trouble he'd caused, and Huck's good cheer vanished. ''Tom, the civilized life just isn't for me. The widow's good to me, but I just can't stand it. I had to leave, Tom, and I'm never going back.''

"Well, that's too bad, Huck," Tom said. He had a plan to make Huck go home. "You see, I've been thinking of starting a gang of robbers. It's great fun to be a robber, you know. I was going to ask you to be in it, but . . ." Tom let his voice trail off.

"Oh, Tom, that would be great!"

"Huck, I can't let you into the gang if you're not respectable."

Huck's face fell. "Can't let me in? Tom, you let me be a pirate!"

"Yes, but that's different. A robber is classier than a pirate.

"Tom, you've always been my friend. You wouldn't leave me out like that, would you?"

"I wouldn't *want* to, but what would people say? 'There goes Tom Sawyer's Gang. He lets pretty low characters in it!' They'd mean you, Huck. I can't have that."

Huck was silent for a moment. Finally, he said, "Well, I'll go back to the widow for a month and see if I can stand it, if you'll let me in your gang."

"All right, Huck, it's a deal. Come on. I'll even ask the widow to let up on you a little."

"Would you? That's good. If she's not so hard on me, I think I can manage. When are you going to start the gang, Tom?"

"Oh, as soon as I can get the boys together."

"Great! I'll be such a good robber, the widow will be proud she took me in," Huck said happily. "Let's go, Tom!"